Silent

illustrated by *Susan Jeffers*

DUTTON CHILDREN'S BOOKS · NEW YORK

Night

verses by *Joseph Mohr*

Library of Congress Cataloging-in-Publication Data
Mohr, Joseph, 1792-1848.
Silent night.
Translation of: Stille Nacht, heilige Nacht.
Summary: An illustrated version of the well-known
German Christmas hymn celebrating the birth of Christ.
I. Christmas music—Texts. [I. Christmas music. 2. Hymns] I. Jeffers, Susan, ill. II Title.
PZ8.3.M717Si 1984 783.6'52 84-8113
ISBN 0-525-47136-7

Published in the United States by Dutton Children's Books,
a division of Penguin Young Readers Group
345 Hudson Street, New York, New York 10014
www.penguinputnam.com
Designed by Beth Herzog
Music engraved by Robert Sherwin
Manufactured in China
1 3 5 7 9 10 8 6 4 2

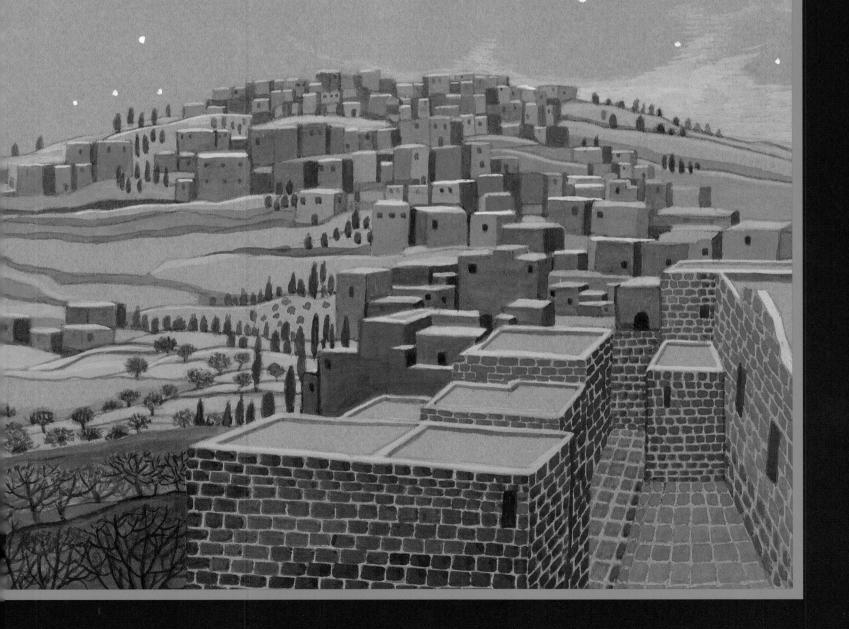

To Aunt Rose and Uncle Tom
S.J.

*S*ilent night, holy night.

*A*ll is calm, all is bright.

Round yon Virgin Mother and Child.
Holy Infant, so tender and mild,
Sleep in heavenly peace.

*S*leep in heavenly peace.

*S*ilent night, holy night!
Shepherds quake at the sight.
Glories stream from heaven afar.

Heav'nly hosts sing "Alleluia!"
Christ the Savior is born!
Christ the Savior is born!

*S*ilent night, holy night!
Guiding star, lend thy light.

_S_ee the Eastern wise men bring
Gifts and homage to our King.

Christ the Savior is here!

Jesus the Savior is here!

Silent Night

verses by Joseph Mohr   *music by Franz Gruber*

1. Si – lent night, ho – ly night. All is calm,
2. Si – lent night, ho – ly night! Shep – herds quake
3. Si – lent night, ho – ly night! Guid – ing star,

all is bright. Round yon Vir – gin Moth – er and Child.
at the sight. Glo – ries stream ___ from heav – en a – far.
lend thy light. See the East – ern wise ___ men bring

Ho – ly In – fant, so ten – der and mild, Sleep in heav – en – ly
Heav'n – ly hosts ___ sing "Al – le – lu – ia!" Christ the Sav – ior is
Gifts and hom – age to ___ our King. Christ the Sav – ior is

peace. _____ Sleep ___ in heav – en – ly peace. _____
born! _____ Christ ___ the Sav – ior is born! _____
here! _____ Je – sus the Sav – ior is here! _____